Untouched

Publication Date: September 10, 2018

AQUARIOTS
U N L I M I T E D

ISBN-13: 978-1-7750252-5-2

Chapter 1

Cerieda was a beautiful princess. Though she was only a child, she was already among the fairest in the kingdom, with her silky golden tresses and gentle green eyes. She was kind and sweet, with grace of character and an innocent nature for which she was beloved by all. As she turned thirteen and began to blossom into womanhood, it became clear that she would only become more lovely with time. Because of this, her father worried for her safety, knowing well the selfish hearts of men. Thence he commissioned her grandfather, a great shaman, to cast a spell of protection over her; this he did while waving a ceremonial staff over her head.

Quoth he,

" 'She shall not be disrobed against her will,

By any man who wish her ill;

Only he with purest heart and intent,

Truest love or heavensent,

May touch her so if she concurs,

That man whose love will be hers.' "

Cerieda felt a cool prickling settle around her like a second skin. In a trice it was gone. Other than that, she didn't feel any different. She went over the words again in her mind, trying to work out what exactly they entailed. Did that mean the spell would physically repel the touch of everyone but her true love? Or only those who had the wrong intentions?

A few weeks later, a debutante ball was held in the palace to celebrate her coming of age. Young princes and princesses from all across the land were invited.

Cerieda stood in front of the full-length mirror in her dressing room, tying her sash. There was a knock on the door.

"Are you ready, Cerieda?" her father called through the wood.

"Just about," she replied, and set her diamond-studded tiara on her head.

She went to open the door, and joined the king in the hall. Even on formal occasions he didn't wear regal robes, simply his usual long coat of embroidered maroon velvet. His crown was a modest band of gold inlaid with a few rubies.

As they turned and headed down the corridor, Cerieda wondered, "If you don't want boys to meet me, why make my appearance at a dance at all?"

"It's not that I don't want them to get to know you," her father said. "I just don't want them trying anything they shouldn't." He gave her a smile behind his short brown beard. "Besides, I do want you to have a good time. You still can, without there being any touching."

The king entered the grand hall first while Cerieda waited outside. Then, a few moments later, she made her entrance into the spacious room, where dozens of brightly-dressed youths were gathered. She was announced by a herald, and the guests greeted her by bowing. Once she'd joined the crowd, the band began playing courtly music.

A slim, sandy-haired prince came up to her and bent at the waist. "Care to dance?" Though his words were polite, his face was set.

She smiled at being asked. "Certainly." They went to the middle of the ballroom floor and faced each other.

He set a hand on her waist, but jerked it back immediately, flapping it in pain. "Ow! I sprained my wrist!" Grimacing, he rubbed it with his other hand.

Cerieda withdrew her hands together in front of her bodice, concerned. "Sorry," she murmured. "It must be the spell Grandfather put on me." Even though the prince had only been assuming the dance form, and it hadn't been without her consent.

The boy looked up at her with a frown. "The what?"

She lowered her eyes, soberly smoothing her skirts. "We can only dance together if we don't touch," she said in an even smaller voice.

He eyed her very oddly sidelong and drifted off – probably to find a less weird partner, or perhaps to nurse his injury.

Head down, Cerieda stepped over to the side of the room to wait for a dance that didn't involve any touching.

When one began, she was approached by a dark-haired prince a little older than her. He bowed to her while she curtsied to him, and then they circled each other, both with one arm upraised, their loosely curled hands hovering an inch apart. For the rest of it they danced around each other with hands behind their backs, or gracefully extended their arms in complementary directions. But even so, Cerieda had to keep any eye out and make sure not to accidentally brush up against any of the other dancers. She didn't want the spell to hurt anyone. It gave her a guilty sense of trepidation in the pit of her stomach to feel dangerous in her own skin.

As she and her dance partner headed toward each other again, she realized the next move was for them to link arms. Her breath caught and she missed a step, but her hesitation didn't come soon enough to prevent him from hooking the crooks of their elbows. They swept about in a circle then disengaged, and Cerieda watched him anxiously for signs of the spell taking effect. When several moments passed and nothing adverse seemed to happen to him, she let out a sigh of relief. Maybe arm-in-arm contact didn't count as him touching her, since it wasn't with his hand.

But as soon as the dance was over, Cerieda returned to the sidelines again and stayed there. There was no point risking the welfare of others just for a little fun.

She sat out that part of any of the subsequent balls she was obligated to be present at, too, though everyone started to find her strange for turning down every request, perhaps even thinking she did it because she didn't consider them good enough for her.

Eventually she told her father that he didn't have to keep hosting balls on her account, since odds were that the one whom the spell didn't apply to wasn't likely to be at the next one any more than at the last.

As Cerieda got older, princes and lordlings kept visiting from neighbouring kingdoms and estates to see the beautiful princess, undoubtedly with the goal of establishing a union between their countries or elevating their own status. A few took liberties with a kiss on her hand or a hand on her knee – but shortly thereafter they each suffered unfortunate mishaps, from taking a falling vase to the head to breaking a finger. One princeling once tried to surreptitiously undo the back of her bodice, and somehow managed to cut his finger on her button; another time a lad reached for her derriere, but his hand inexplicably cramped up an inch away from it. Other such attempts were always met with similarly painful or deflective occurrences, and before long the legend of the curse was born.

As it became widespread, the string of suitors dwindled to a stop. The king considered it for the better, since those types clearly weren't in it for the right reasons. Cerieda wasn't so sure. She certainly hadn't appreciated the others trying to take advantage of her, but she didn't want to believe they were all like that. What if these rumours kept away the right one, too?

Chapter 2

Cerieda slowly walked along through the gardens of the palace, gazing down at her hands, folded at her waist. Her twentieth birthday had come and gone, and she was still alone. Many princesses younger than her were already married, or at least in a courtship.

Her peridot-green skirts of silk whispered as she moved. Like the sweet nothings that no one would ever get close enough to whisper in her ear. Aching welled in her heart. She was so lonely. She longed for the touch of a man, to be held and loved, to be able to share with him all the love she had inside. But every prince, every lord, every courtier, every male she ever encountered knew the legend, and avoided her like she was infectious, circumventing a wide space around her whenever they passed. At best they smiled at her and gave a shallow bow, hands tucked safely behind their backs.

She had never been kissed, never held hands, never been romantically embraced, never even been caressed in the slightest. What few suitors she'd had over the years had always stayed a generous distance from her, but since there was no foreseeable advancement to the relationship, they'd all promptly discontinued it.

How was she to know who was meant for her, when no one would risk getting near her? If everyone were to simply give her a tap of the finger, then it

12

would only be a matter of waiting to see who *wasn't* affected by the curse. But they'd never willingly endanger themselves like that – nor did she wish such harm on any of them. Cerieda let out a quiet sigh. Sometimes she wondered if her father had, however inadvertently, condemned her to a life of forlorn solitude.

Cerieda turned down another walkway. The gardens spread extensively behind the north side of the palace, divided into four quarters, with many paths winding through them. She often came out here, where there were fewer people she had to steer clear of – save for the occasional groundskeeper who was there to water the plants or trim the many hedges and topiaries and ornamental saplings. Varnished benches sat at convenient intervals, under a shady tree, in a secluded nook, or facing a particularly scenic view. There was the occasional marble statue of a rearing horse or a swan with uplifted wings, each up on a tall plinth. The elaborate landscaping included all the showiest blooms – coral-pink carnations and sunny daffodils, yellow lilies and white roses and red tulips, all filling the air with their sweet fragrances. It gave her some peace of mind, to just see and smell the flowers – the only things that didn't shy away from her.

Once the afternoon began to turn into evening, Cerieda headed back into the palace. As she proceeded down the hallways of polished stone tiles, she passed several maidservants in simple grey livery. They didn't have to evade her like the men did, but it wasn't their place to get too close to the princess either. She'd occasionally tried to befriend some of the maids who were her age, but they only ever treated her with the respect owed to a superior, not considering themselves her equal. The only other girls she knew were the princesses of other kingdoms, but they only visited a few times a year for social events; not often enough to become close with them.

Cerieda overheard some of the servants gossiping. "...it'll be good to have guests around here again..."

"...I hear the nobleman is quite handsome..."

"Oh, Princess, the king wants to see you," the headmatron remarked to Cerieda as she went by.

With a nod, Cerieda continued to the throne room and turned in through the wide archway. The seat on the low dais ahead wasn't so much a throne as a large chair carved of cherrywood, with inset red upholstery on the seat and back and top of the armrests. The king rarely ever sat in it except on the most official of occasions; he was more often working at his desk off to one side.

Her father spotted her as she came in. "Ah, Cerieda! There you are." He beckoned with an outspread arm. "A nobleman and his scribes arrived today from the northwest kingdom. They'll be staying here for some time while the scribes make copies of several volumes in our library. He graciously offered to have his estate give us rare goods in exchange. It would've been good if you were here to welcome them with me."

She held back a sigh. "Perhaps it's just as well. Being introduced to me might only have driven them away."

The king's face softened with sympathy. "I'm sorry this spell is hard on you. But I did it for your protection."

Cerieda nodded solemnly. "I know, Father."

He gave her a comforting hug, and she put her arms around him too. At least she could still be close with her family. She wondered if he still would've had the spell put on her if it meant he'd never be able to hold his own daughter again either.

The king backed up. "Dinner will be served in about an hour. I'll see you there?"

"Yes. I'll just do some reading until then."

Cerieda went back out into the hall and continued up it until she reached the door to her quarters, on the right. Entering the dimly firelit room, she passed the side of her bed and settled herself in an armchair beside the hearth, curling up with a book of romance. One time, when her father had come upon her reading one such story, he'd expressed concern that it wasn't something he'd necessarily recommend, since it might just make her even more sorely wistful for something she didn't yet have. Which was true, but sometimes it also made her feel better for a while, to vicariously experience the characters falling and being in love, to read about tender kisses and gentle caresses — to become momentarily lost in imagination of another life.

Chapter 3

Cerieda was strolling through the gardens again a few days later. Nearing the point where four walkways met, she lifted her head when she noticed a man coming her way, regarding the flowers. His neat brown hair had a hint of auburn, and he was dressed in a handsome coat befitting a minor nobleman.

He glanced up, and paused when he saw her. "Oh. Good afternoon."

She smiled politely as she came to a stop at the crossroad too. "Afternoon."

"You must be Cerieda. I'm Danavan. I'm having my scribes make copies of some books in the library."

She inclined her head in greeting, but kept her hands folded at her waist. "Welcome to our residence. Forgive me if I don't offer my hand, but I wouldn't want you to be affected by the spell."

His face showed a little concern. "Ah, yes, I've heard."

Cerieda felt like sighing. But she shouldn't be surprised that the word had spread that far, too.

Danavan looked away. "I was heading to see the north garden. Which path were you taking?"

A courteous way to check that their routes didn't overlap. "The same. But I can choose another."

"Oh, no, don't think of it!" he protested. "This is your home – you have the freedom to go where you wish; I'm just the guest here."

Of course; since he was a gentleman, he'd offer to change course himself.

"I'll just accompany you, so long as you don't mind," Danavan finished.

Cerieda flicked her eyes to him at the unexpected suggestion, and cocked her head. "Not at all." They turned and started up the northward walkway. Danavan kept a generous gap between them, his hands clasped behind his back. Cerieda was still considering him. "You're not averse to being near me? Most men make themselves scarce as soon as they hear I'm the one with the curse."

He looked over at her with a quizzically furrowed brow. "Why would I? It's hardly your fault. And I'm sure you have a lovely personality – you deserve companionship as much as anyone else."

Her heart warmed with grateful

appreciation. He was the first man to see it that way. Cerieda turned her head away, watching the stones pass beneath her feet. "Are you liking your stay here?"

"Oh, yes, you have a very splendid home," he replied, admiring the scenery around them. "You should be famous not only for your library, but your gardens as well."

"Did you find all the books you needed there?"

"Even more than I'd hoped for. You have a truly impressive collection. There were several rare volumes I was keen to finally get hold of; *The Workings of Motion and Matter*, *The Explorer's Guide to All the Lands*, *The History of Magic*."

"And why are you looking to copy those? To add to your personal collection?"

"More than that, I intend to make more copies at my estate, then distribute them to other towns and kingdoms. I travel to many places for this same purpose. My goal is to spread knowledge to as many people as possible."

Cerieda studied him with growing admiration. "That's very commendable of you."

Danavan bowed his head. "But I must confess, my interest isn't limited to only the informative texts. I found myself perusing some of the works of fiction here, too. I never can seem to resist re-reading Therion's *Quintessence*."

Her interest sparked up at hearing one of her favourites. " 'For what are we without the ideals that make us strive'," she quoted.

He looked over at her in delight. "You know it, too?"

Cerieda smiled wryly. "Those books have kept me company more often than people."

"Right – you've had access to that library all your life. I wish I could've grown up with such an extensive collection." Danavan gazed off into the distance. "I found it particularly moving when Lucerna throws her mirror into the lake, but the water itself still reflects her face."

"I think it represents letting go of her obsession with how others see her. And in so doing, she discovers her true identity."

His expression was impressed. "That's remarkably insightful."

They arrived at the northern garden, where there were white roses and stone birdbaths and marble statues. They talked for a while more, until a servant came to inform them that the midday meal was about to be served. Danavan walked Cerieda back to the palace. Then, after cordial goodbyes, they parted ways, since the royal family didn't customarily dine with guests on a daily basis.

Over the next while, the two of them came upon each other every now and then, as was to be expected when staying in the same place. Danavan always stopped to say hello, and also engaged her in pleasant conversation whenever they were in each other's company for long, whether they were heading down the same hallway or browsing a shelf in the library or having tea in the parlour. They discussed art and music and literature, statecraft and history and everything in between. It was always a riveting exchange of thoughts and ideas, and they found they shared many perspectives. Cerieda was glad to have someone to talk to — someone who treated her like she was a normal person. Danavan even started coming to see her each day, seemingly for no other reason than to spend longer amounts of time with her. She suspected he might even be asking the servants where she was, to keep finding her so consistently. Of course, there were only so many places she was likely to be.

On one such occasion, he met up with her in the garden and asked if he could join her.

"You have no other business to attend to?" Cerieda teased.

Danavan smiled ruefully. "Well, no, since I've already made my treaty with the king and pointed out the tomes to copy. I'm no scribe; they're the ones who'll do the rest from here, but it could take weeks."

"Then couldn't they do it without you?"

"I could return to my estate, yes, but it wouldn't be right to leave them here unsupervised. I ought to stay and make sure they get the work done. Besides, I'm here to see the sights in this kingdom. That's why I love to travel."

Cerieda settled down onto a bench, and Danavan lowered himself a respectful distance beside her.

"I have to admit, you're rather the main attraction." As she raised her eyebrow at the odd turn of phrase, he went on, "After all those years hearing about the untouchable princess, it's almost like meeting a celebrity."

She smiled bashfully and turned away. "Living under a curse is hardly glamorous."

Danavan studied her intently.

"Have you ever tried to break the spell? There must be some kind of book on the subject."

She looked at him curiously, wondering why he would ask. "My grandfather made it specifically for me. As far as I know, there's never been another one exactly like it before."

"What were the words, exactly? If you don't mind my asking."

Suppressing a trace of abashment, Cerieda repeated them to him. She'd come to memorize it by now, after recalling it dozens of times to make sure she knew how to best avoid inadvertent triggers of it.

Danavan rubbed his chin. "Are there any loopholes? If the suitor were to wear gloves, perhaps?"

She shook her head. "It isn't dependent on direct skin contact. Whether it's through a glove or a sleeve or both, it still takes effect."

"What if it was only a gesture of true friendship? Such as a pat on the back or a hug of congratulations?"

Cerieda smiled sadly. "I've yet to find out. None of the boys I've met seemed interested in being my friend."

There was a trace of sympathy in his eyes. His gaze drifted away, and then he brightened. "How about an act of selfless preservation? Say, if you tripped and he had to catch you? I can't imagine any self-respecting gentleman would be so wary of the curse as to let a lady fall to the ground."

She turned thoughtful. "The spell doesn't say anything about that. But I haven't encountered such a situation, either."

A mischievous smile started

spreading across his face, and she eyed him.

"What?"

Danavan looked away innocently. "I won't suggest an experiment. I doubt it would work the same if it was planned in advance, anyway." He drummed his fingers on his knee. "Has anyone ever bumped into you by accident? Did the curse apply to them, too?"

Cerieda thought back. "That did happen once, years ago, with one of the new servants in the hallway. But nothing consequential seemed to come of it. He considered himself lucky to escape unscathed. The spell mostly has to do with the hands and whether it's done deliberately."

Danavan squinted shrewdly. "What if you were the one who did the touching? Technically, the spell doesn't forbid that."

She eyed him sidelong. "You have a great deal of questions."

He dipped his head sheepishly. "My apologies. I'm just fascinated by your condition."

"Indeed? Most men find it quite the opposite."

Danavan grinned. "Call it my studious nature. And you still haven't answered my question."

Cerieda became introspective. "Well, I've never tried, since I wouldn't want to cause misfortune to them if it didn't work." Her face grew a little warmer, but she continued with the indelicate subject, phrasing it unobtrusively. "Even if I could, it would surely prompt them to reciprocate, and that would still activate the curse. Besides, there's never been anyone I've wanted to get close to." She lowered her eyes. "Much as I wish there was," she added in a whisper. Loneliness welled up in her again as she remembered how she might well always be alone, and she sighed. "Is there something else we could discuss?"

Danavan watched her with commiserative concern. "Of course. I didn't mean to bring up any source of distress."

"I know. It's just that trying to find loopholes made me realize there are none."

"But at least it was fun to speculate for a while there, wasn't it?"

That got a faint smile out of her. It *was* nice to have someone to talk to about it. She couldn't voice her woes to her father, of course, not when he was the one who had sanctioned the spell. And she couldn't discuss loopholes with her grandfather, since he wouldn't want her looking for any in his spell.

Danavan's face became earnest again. "Don't despair, Cerieda. The right man for you is out there somewhere; the spell said so. There's still time."

She looked over at him. Lifting the corner of her mouth in appreciation, she nodded.

Chapter 4

Danavan sat across from Cerieda, playing a game of court at a table in the garden. He wasn't usually so engaged by it, but she was quite a good player.

"What's it like in the northwest kingdom?" she asked conversationally. "Is your estate doing well?"

"Oh, yes, business is good. But to be honest, I'm glad to get a little time away from it." He moved his granite duke piece one square forward, toward her alabaster countess.

She dodged it sideways behind her own jester to prevent him from cornering it. "Something troubling you there?"

Danavan considered his next move. "Well, there are these two farmers on my land," he began. "They've been quarrelling for the longest time. They expect me to resolve it for them, of course. They can't agree on the location of the boundary line between their two fields. Their forefathers founded the farms using a stream to mark the middle of it. But apparently that stream has changed course over the generations, and now it's running through the corner of the second man's farm. The first farmer claims he owns everything up to the western bank, as per the agreement. The other man argues he's entitled to the same amount of land he's always had."

He advanced his earl nearer her baron, but she brought her duchess out from the other side in the direction of his, so he had to whisk his page across two diagonal spaces to come between them.

As Cerieda took her turn again, Danavan went on, "I've considered dividing their properties equally with a fence in the exact middle – but then the first man would no longer have access to the water at all. Or I could officially make the division down the middle of the stream, but then the second farmer would still have the smaller parcel of land." He sighed. "I just don't know what to do about it." He retreated his count behind her herald to avoid being confronted by her marquess.

"Maybe you could divide the land diagonally," Cerieda suggested absently.

He paused, then looked up at her in amazement. "That's brilliant." The farmers would each get half the stream, and yet both their acreage would be the same.

She smiled slightly as she moved her piece. "I learned a few things from my father."

"Well, you're certainly better at mediation than I," Danavan remarked. He waited until her hand was well away from the board before he reached out himself and made his next play.

Cerieda studied the layout for a moment, then took hold of a figure, but hesitated, slowly tapping a slender finger on top of it.

After a minute, he glanced up at her expectantly. "Are you going to make your move?" he prompted.

She met his eyes, a teasing twinkle in her own. "Are you sure you want me to?"

Danavan showed a bit of a smile. "By all means."

She set her emperor down in front

of his prince, thus blocking all his royal pieces with her own and bringing the game to an impasse. He stared at the board, wondering how she'd gotten that past him. Cerieda folded her hands in her lap. "Pardon me for winning. It's in poor taste to best a guest at a game."

But he watched her complacently. "Oh, I hardly mind." It was just another indication of her impressive intellect, and he could hardly hold it against her when she'd just used that same mind to give him an offhand solution to his longstanding problem.

As Danavan was heading to his guest quarters in the palace, he saw the king coming his way. "Your Highness," Danavan greeted smoothly, bowing. He'd exchanged pleasantries in passing with the king before, and even dined with him a few times, and he seemed to find Danavan a likeable guest.

"Ah, Danavan." The king came to a stop before him. "I hear you've been spending time with my daughter." The words gave Danavan a twinge of apprehension in spite of himself. "You're keeping your conduct agreeable, I trust?"

He smiled easily. "Oh, yes, all we do is talk. Cerieda is a scintillating conversationalist. I would never try anything untoward. The spell would surely deter me if I did!"

The king beamed in approval, and clapped him on the shoulder. He was more informal than most kings, but then his was a lesser kingdom than the others. Or perhaps it was because Danavan was only a minor nobleman, not a man of equal rank. "It's good of you to keep her company. There have been so few who were gentlemanly enough to do so."

"It's no trouble at all, I assure you."

The king gave a nod and continued on past him to let him go on his way.

Danavan was walking with Cerieda again through the gardens the next day.

Looking down at the flowers, she tenderly touched a lily petal as she passed, then let her hand trail along the tall grasses. She was so graceful, so beautiful. She had so much gentleness in her, so much love that she wanted to share even with the plants. It was clear why she was considered the fairest princess in the land. Just the sight of her always filled his heart with adoration.

Cerieda paused to bend and take in the aroma of a tulip. When they came near a tree, she went to stand beside it, and put her arms around its trunk like it was a column – or a friend. She tilted the side of her head onto it and smiled at Danavan.

He couldn't help smiling with amusement too. It was a very odd thing to see a princess doing. "You hug a lot of trees?"

"At least they don't mind." She gazed up at the branches. "But it's something I would do, even if it weren't for the spell. Everything deserves to be appreciated."

His admiration for her deepened. It was just like her to have that kind of compassionate outlook. Seeing her soft figure resting against the bole, Danavan almost wished he was the tree.

As the weeks went on, his respect and fondness for her only grew, and he always looked forward to seeing her. She was the highlight of his day. Even when they were apart, he couldn't stop thinking about her, and about her spell, trying to figure out if there was something he could do for her. Then a thought came to him.

The spell only meant she couldn't hug a *person...*

He promptly went to the nearest town and sought out a pedigree dog breeder. Money was no object for Danavan. He bought a silky black shepherd dog and brought him back to the palace.

Danavan came in the back entrance, but stopped in the doorway when the eager dog tugged forward to the end of his leash. Danavan had to maintain a hold on it to keep him in check.

Cerieda was coming up the hall toward them. "Who is this?" she greeted in delight, kneeling to smooth a hand over the dog's head. He nosed at her cheek, tail wagging so enthusiastically his whole body waggled.

"His name is Midnight. He's for you," Danavan said, and Cerieda looked up at him in wonder. "I figured, at least with him, you could have a companion with whom you can share affection freely."

Bowing her head, she looked into the dog's eyes, tousling her hands over his fur. "You are so *sweet*," she cooed.

Danavan slid his hands into his pockets. "The breeder assures me that he's the friendliest, quietest purebred in the kennel."

She glanced up at Danavan with a small smile. "I didn't mean the dog," she murmured warmly.

His mouth slowly spread into a smile too.

Cerieda kept stroking Midnight, and even wrapped her arms around his neck in a hug.

Danavan smiled wider. It did his heart good to see her expressing her warmth without inhibition. *And then*

44

whenever you're with him, you'll think of me.

The king came in from an archway, and paused when he saw the dog. "What's this?" There was clear disapproval in his tone. He glanced at Danavan, then back to Midnight. "Such a rambunctious playmate is hardly fit for a princess," he objected.

Dismay tweaked Danavan. He hadn't considered whether the king would oppose it.

"Oh, Father, please let me keep him," Cerieda pleaded. "It would mean so much to me."

The king watched her hugging the dog for a moment; then his face softened into an indulgent smile. "Very well. Anything for you, Cerieda." She beamed with gratitude. "But he'll have to be housed in the servants' quarters. I don't want him running loose in the palace."

"Of course." Cerieda got up and started heading down the hall, still looking over her shoulder at Midnight. She patted a hand on the side of her skirt. "Come on, Midnight!" she invited, and the dog readily bounded along beside her.

Smiling, Danavan turned down a side passage.

Chapter 5

Danavan strolled alongside Cerieda through the summer air of the gardens. He'd been there almost a month, though it seemed like it'd gone by all too soon.

"So, how are the scribes coming along?" she prompted. "Are they just about done?" She sounded almost like she'd be disappointed if that was the case.

He kept his voice casual. "Yes, but I assigned them a few more, smaller books. I figured I might as well get some of my favourites down while we're here." He proffered a smile. In actuality, he'd done it just so he would have a reason to remain that much longer.

Cerieda seemed to brighten a little. "Oh." Her tone was more hopeful. They settled onto a bench. "I think this is a record for how long I've known someone since the spell was enacted," she remarked lightly.

Danavan started mustering his courage. "I have to say, I admire your fortitude, living with the spell without even becoming bitter about it. I can't imagine what it must be like."

Cerieda lowered her eyes. "It hasn't been easy. But I've made my peace with it."

He wanted so much to comfort her, to put an arm around her shoulders, or just to show her how he felt about her. But he couldn't. Danavan turned his face away, and saw a yellow lily that stood beside his knee. He picked it, intending to gift it to Cerieda. But then he had a thought. Holding it by the end of the stem, he lowered it so the flowerhead trailed across the back of her hand. Cerieda looked at it, then lifted her eyes to him. No harm came to him, since it didn't count as him touching her. Lifting the flower, Danavan stroked its soft petals along her cheek in lieu of a tender hand. "Look at that, I found a loophole," he murmured.

Her eyes softened, and a trace of pink rose to her cheeks. But she didn't move away. He offered her the lily, and she accepted it gingerly, careful not to let her fingers brush his while taking hold of the stem. Cerieda bowed her head over it, inhaling its scent. It was such a feminine pose.

A wavy lock of hair slid down by her cheek, making the image even more perfect. And yet he felt an urge to tuck it back for her.

Danavan folded his elbow up on the back of the bench. "Does hair qualify as part of the spell?" he whispered.

Cerieda turned her head slightly to eye him past the kiss curl. "It might not," she admitted, sounding curious to find out.

The amplitude of his emotions made him daring. Very carefully, he reached a hand out, well above her shoulder, and took the end of the strand between his first two fingers. Cerieda stayed still, watching him. When there was no repercussion, not even so much as a static shock, he drew the strand back and looped it behind her ear. Then, unable to resist, he sank his hand into the back of her thick golden hair, gently closing his fingers around it, without getting near her neck. Her tresses were soft and warm and smooth. It had him breathing deeply, just to hold a part of her, however innocuous – to have his hand that much closer to her face.

His heart was so full. Even this brief contact nearly made it overflow. Danavan slowly withdrew his arm and clasped his hands together, before he could be tempted to do more.

"How's Midnight doing?" he asked, still softly.

Cerieda gave him a warm smile. "He's a dear. I can't thank you enough. It's the most considerate thing anyone's done for me." Still meeting his eyes, she traced a finger along the edge of one of the lily petals. "And I want you to know, I'm grateful for all the time you've spent with me. I've never had so good a friend as you."

Danavan slowly smiled, and nodded a little. But even at the same time as his heart was warmed by her sentiment, there was a trace of resignation in the pit of his stomach. She, in her innocence, probably saw him as nothing more than a friend. And why wouldn't she, when he was nothing special, and she deserved so much better? He shouldn't compromise that by implying he had deeper feelings for her than that. Besides, what hope did he have? He couldn't truly act on it anyway, not with the curse.

Late that night, Danavan took a walk in the empty hallways, deep in thought. *What am I to do?* He was in love with Cerieda – there was no mistaking it. But he could never actually touch her. *Leave it to me and my romantic folly to fall for the only girl in the land who's utterly off-limits.* They had no future together. How could they, when he would never be able to fully express his affection for her, not even with a hug or a hand on hers? Their relationship could never be more than it was now: being in each other's company, talking, engaging in pastimes together – but always an inch apart.

Furthermore, he couldn't stay here in the palace forever. He'd already extended his visit longer than he'd planned. He would have to be leaving soon. And then he wouldn't even get to see her anymore. *Should I tell her how I feel before I leave?* Danavan ruminated on that, but ultimately decided against it, with some dejection. It would probably just cause her unnecessary distress.

But if he did let her know, could he chance one intimate moment with her before he went out of her life? Or if he stayed, was there any way to make it work? Would it be worth suffering a few injuries, if it meant he'd get to hold her, to kiss her? The more liberties he took, the worse the repercussions might be. But if they only happened once after each act, perhaps he could just recover in between, as long as it wasn't too severe.

But no. If she didn't feel the same, he would never try to take it further. He would just have to cherish what time he had left with her, then go back to his kingdom and hope that, somehow, time and distance would dilute his memory of her and lessen his heartbreak.

A stifling tension banded his chest. His desperation to hold back the anguish made it seem hard to breathe. He felt trapped amidst heat and aggravation, even while stubborn resistance churned within him. He didn't want to stop loving her. He didn't think he could. Why should he have to, when she was so deserving of love, when sharing that love with her was supposed to be a good thing?

He surely wasn't the first man to fall for her. With her kind green eyes, her gentle nature, all of her shaped and proportioned perfectly... But there was no reason to think that such an exceptional woman as her would love an ordinary man like him.

As Danavan neared the royal wing, he noticed that the door to Cerieda's chambers stood ajar. He drifted to a stop outside it. Torchlight spilled into the room, dimly illuminating Cerieda's blanketed form. Affection welled in him. He slipped in, just to look upon her for a moment. She lay asleep in the silken sheets of her luxurious bed, her head partly turned away. Danavan softly stepped closer, and knelt by her side.

Her golden tresses fanned out on the pillow around her head like the rays of the rising sun. Her hair smelled like daffodils in the morning light. Danavan leaned forward, extending a hand toward her sweet face. He paused a hair's breadth from her cheek, yearning so much to touch that smooth, fair skin. But he hesitated, sighing inwardly, knowing well the consequences.

Cerieda stirred ever so slightly, turning her head so that his suspended fingers brushed her cheek. Danavan withdrew his hand with a silent gasp, and looked at it in wonder. A thrill of hope rose in his heart, but it was soon replaced by wariness as he stood, glancing about the dark room, then went back out the door.

From then on he went around

tense and alert for signs of his impending doom, eyeing every gardener with a pair of shears that might trip toward him, on the lookout for any brick that might come loose and catch him on the head. He also avoided Cerieda with a will, lest he accidentally come into contact with her again and worsen his fate. But the days went on, and nothing terrible befell him, nothing at all out of the ordinary – not so much as a stubbed toe.

At last Danavan slowed down and began to wonder – could this mean...he was the one man who was exempt from the curse? The one she truly loved, as much as he loved her – the only one she could ever be with?

Surely that was too much to hope. Maybe it just didn't count as an infraction, because he hadn't been the one to initiate the touch.

But if there was any chance for him, he couldn't give up until he found out for sure — even if it meant risking a little injury.

Chapter 6

Cerieda paced along the corridor, a trace of worry in her heart. Danavan hadn't come to see her in days. A few times, she thought she'd even glimpsed him just before he dodged out of sight, as if he was deliberately avoiding her. *Have I finally scared him off?* She didn't want to lose his friendship, even if they could never be more than that. She didn't think she could bear it if the only man she'd gotten close to were to shut her out too.

She knew Danavan would have to return to his own kingdom before long. But Cerieda was hoping that perhaps they could at least exchange correspondences by letter after that, and still continue their association that way. She hadn't yet suggested it to him, since she didn't want to seem presumptuous.

She was missing him already, even after so short a time apart. She'd enjoyed every minute they were together. He was so ingenious, finding little ways around her spell, ones that even she hadn't been looking for. No other man had cared enough to bother. Buying her a dog she could hug, stroking her with a flower... She remembered how it had trailed tingles across her skin. And when he'd touched her hair...it had been such an intimate moment. She welcomed the gesture when it came from Danavan. Her heart filled with warmth just thinking about him. She'd never felt this for anyone else before. She couldn't imagine going back to a life without him.

What if she was falling for him even when he wasn't the one the spell referred to? Was that even possible? Could they be doomed to be tragic lovers who could never be together? That would be too cruel.

At last, she spotted Danavan in the hall ahead, walking slowly with his back to her.

"Danavan," she greeted softly as she came up behind him, and he turned abruptly, sidestepping so he was out of the way. "I haven't seen you in a while," she went on with some concern. "Is everything all right?"

He looked glad to see her. "There's something I want to test. It might be a risk, but I don't care at this point." He reached for her hand, but she reflexively lifted it back.

"What...?" she breathed, aghast. "You shouldn't – you know what will happen." She very much didn't want him to get hurt because of her curse.

Danavan gave her a slight smile. "Bear with me. I don't think it will." And he gently took her hand in his own. Cerieda drew in a breath. He stroked his other hand atop hers, surrounding it in his warm hold. His hands were so manly, yet cradled hers with such caring.

She looked at their hands in wonder. No dire result was afflicting Danavan. "How can it be...?"

"How I've longed to tell you. I'm in love with you, Cerieda. Deeply and truly."

Her heart skipped a beat, and she lifted her gaze to his. It was more than she could've hoped for. She was filled with such affection and gratitude that her eyes almost misted up. "Oh, Danavan," she whispered. "You're my first and only love."

Relieved adoration came over his face. He tenderly set his hand on her cheek, and Cerieda felt a surge of sweet yearning to finally be touched like that. Squeezing her eyes closed, she leaned into his palm. It was all so overwhelming. Danavan was the exception to the spell after all! She was so indescribably glad it was him, and not someone else.

Cerieda gazed up at him again. Danavan lightly ran his hand down her arm to hold her other hand in his. "You'll never have to be alone again," he said softly.

Warmth rose to her cheeks. She dearly appreciated his words. "You'll stay?"

Danavan smiled. "Of course. Even magic spells couldn't keep me away."

Cerieda grinned. "I'm so happy it turned out to be you. We must tell my family!" she enthused. She turned and hastened down the hallway along with him, holding her skirt clear with one hand as she headed to the throne room.

"Father, look!" she called as she hurried in, and the king glanced up. "I've found the one the spell spoke of! It's Danavan!" As they came to a stop, she held Danavan's hand in hers, linking fingers with it and lifting it up for her father to see. Danavan watched her with a contented expression.

The king looked from one to the other, but when the curse didn't take effect, his face bloomed into a beam. "This is phenomenal!" he exclaimed, spreading his arms as he came over to them. Cerieda's grandfather drifted in the archway at the back corner of the room, likely to investigate the commotion. The king looked over his shoulder at him, and beckoned. "Come see! Is this really the right one?"

Studying Danavan, the shaman crossed to them, his staff clicking on the floor. He was thin and slightly stooped under his robes, with a wiry grey beard and long hair below his bald pate. When he arrived before Danavan and Cerieda, he wove his staff over their heads, squinting searchingly. "The spell is still in place. It will continue to apply to everyone else. But it has indeed recognized him as the only one who was ever meant to be exempt from it." He smiled too.

Cerieda and Danavan shared an exuberant glance.

"Well, I'll be!" the king remarked. "And he was right here all this time!" Then he eyed Danavan closely, and lowered his voice. "Just because you *can* do anything with her now, I hope it doesn't mean you *have...?*"

"Oh, no, Father, we only just found out!" Cerieda dismissed lightly.

The king studied both of them for a moment, then nodded, his expression clearing. He turned his attention back to Danavan. "Well, Danavan, now that you know, what do you intend to do next?"

Danavan looked over at Cerieda with tender eyes and a warm smile. "Marry her, of course," he murmured.

A soft gasp escaped her, and she gazed at him in delight.

"That is, if you'll have me," he added. "Forgive me, I meant to ask you more formally."

"Oh, of course I'll marry you!" Cerieda breathed, turning to him and taking hold of his other hand too.

The king set a hand on each of their backs. "Then I can have no objections. Will you be wanting to hold the wedding here in the palace?"

Cerieda brightened. "That would be great." She looked at Danavan to check with him.

"Sounds good to me," he agreed, then promptly turned and towed her out the archway. "Let's go pick out which room to use!"

She was in just as much of a breathless whirl as he, but she managed to hang back on his hand to pause him in the hallway. "But wait, we should take a moment to plan first, since we're about to spend our life together!" Danavan turned back to her with a twinkle in his eye. "Where shall we live?" It was customary for the man to whisk his bride off to his land, but in this case Cerieda was the one with the higher royal status, so she could hardly leave the kingdom she might have to rule one day. Besides, she didn't think her father would appreciate it, either.

Danavan considered her, then smiled. "I wouldn't want to steal you away from the palace, especially when my manor isn't nearly as grand. But perhaps it'd still be better for us to have a home of our own. I'm sure there's some lovely mansion near here that we can settle into."

Cerieda beamed. "I think I know just the place." Then she became earnest with some concern. "But what of your estate?"

"Oh, I can have my steward manage things there. And maybe I'll visit from time to time to check in on the place, for a change of scenery." Danavan smiled wider. "In fact, I'd like for you to see it sometime."

Chapter 7

Cerieda and Danavan stopped by different parts of the palace, looking around in first the parlour then the gardens, and settled on the grand hall for the location of the ceremony.

That afternoon, they took a carriage to see the mansion Cerieda had in mind. It was just five hours away to the northwest, halfway between the palace and Danavan's kingdom. It was owned by her cousin, but she only frequented it in the summer. She was there at the time, and they discussed the possibility with her while taking a tour of the sunny interior and grounds, which they both thought would be perfect for them. Since Cerieda's cousin was an incurable romantic, she readily agreed to the idea of offering them a marital home as a wedding gift.

They returned to the palace, and the next day, they met with the king again in the throne room, where he was conferring with his advisor and Cerieda's grandfather. They told the king of their plans and that they were ready to get married at the soonest opportunity.

"Don't you feel you're perhaps rushing into this?" the king put forward.

"Why wait?" Cerieda countered blithely. "The spell proves we're meant for each other. We've already known each other for a month."

"And we're quite in love," Danavan added warmly, and she smiled broadly at him in agreement.

"And my closest family is right here." She paused. "Oh. Although, wouldn't you want your own family to attend, Danavan?"

He glanced up in abrupt recollection. "Ah, yes, I suppose it would be good if they were here to see it. I can just send them invitations, while the other preparations are underway." He gave her a brief beam. "It won't take them long to arrive."

"Who will officiate?" the advisor prompted.

The king looked at Cerieda. "Why not your grandfather?" he suggested. "As a shaman, he's qualified to serve in that capacity."

She nodded thoughtfully. "It would be nice to keep it in the family." But then she eyed her grandfather shrewdly. "As long as you don't try to slip any more spells in there," she warned playfully.

71

He showed a bit of an impish smile. "Are you sure? I could easily whip up a complementary one for Danavan that deters women. You'd make a matching couple."

"Oh, Grandfather, don't even suggest!" Cerieda protested with a laugh.

"It won't be needed, anyway," Danavan put in, smiling gently over at Cerieda. "You're the only woman for me."

Her heart warmed, and she lowered her eyes with bashful pleasure.

Danavan sent his scribes back to his estate with the copied books and letters to be delivered by courier from there to his family. Cerieda's father invited distant relatives, as well as dignitaries from all across the land, including the princes and lords that had once attempted to court her, so as to show everyone that the spell had worked. The king also took it upon himself to arrange every detail of the ceremony, sparing no expense to make it as lavish an event for Cerieda as could be.

Other than being consulted on a few decisions, such as what bridal dress she wanted made, she and Danavan mostly had the time to themselves. Cerieda did notice the chamberlain always keeping an eye on the two of them, to make sure they were never alone together for too long; undoubtedly by her father's request. But it wasn't called for; they never did much more than hold hands.

Sometimes, when they stood looking into each other's eyes in a secluded hallway, Danavan would stroke a gentle hand on her shoulder...or her elbow...or the side of her neck, acclimatizing her to his touch, little by little. Every caress let her feel how much he loved her, and made her adore him all the more.

The most it led up to was when Danavan enfolded her in an embrace, and she looped her arms about his neck. He drew her closer by the waist like he never wanted to let go, nestling his head beside hers. Being in a hug with Danavan was entirely different experience. It made her warm all over. With their hearts right near each other, it filled hers with devoted contentment.

Finally, the week of waiting passed, and the wedding took place in the grand hall, which was festooned with golden draperies and dozens of glowing candelabras. The guests sat on benches that had been brought in for the purpose, facing where Cerieda stood with Danavan before her grandfather. Midnight even sat at the front, upon Cerieda's insistence. A servant boy had his arm around the silky dog's back to keep him there.

Her grandfather began speaking. "Today we are gathered here to celebrate the happiness that these two people have found. The spell placed on Princess Cerieda was designed to thwart any man who is not her true love. It has proven its worth twofold, for now it has verified the identity of the one who was always meant for her. This union is attended by magic, for there is none more powerful than true love."

Danavan and Cerieda turned to each other. She had her hands folded before her skirt; his were clasped behind his back. Danavan didn't take his eyes off hers.

The shaman went on, "Danavan, since you wish to become Cerieda's husband, you will be obliged to love her and only her, to support and respect her, for all your life. Will you take this vow as your own?"

Danavan's gaze was full of love. "I will."

"Cerieda, since you wish to become Danavan's wife, you will be obliged to love him and only him, to support and respect him, for all your life. Will you take this vow as your own?"

She could scarcely contain her ebullience. It was hard to believe it had only been a month ago that she'd thought she'd never find love, and now she was about to be married to Danavan. "I will."

"Then, with my power as a shaman, in the presence of magic, the king, and your kinfolk, I declare that the two of you are hereupon united in matrimony. You may now kiss the princess."

Danavan gently set his hands on either side of Cerieda's face, stroking his thumbs there, and gave her a small smile. Her cheeks grew warmer at his touch, and her heart started beating faster in anticipation. Then Danavan slowly leaned in, tilting his head, and tenderly kissed her. Cerieda inhaled with the sweet thrill that rose in her. Her lips tingled; it felt so foreign, but so gratifying, to have his face so close, his lips surrounding hers. She absently rested light hands on his chest.

When Danavan backed away to meet her eyes again, Cerieda's heart leapt at the realization they were officially married. It was a great comfort to know they'd have a lifetime to hold each other. And Cerieda quivered with excitement to think that after tonight, there wasn't a single part of her that would remain untouched.

The End